The Big Bunny
and the Easter Eggs

by Steven Kroll

illustrated by Janet Stevens

SCHOLASTIC INC.
New York Toronto London Auckland Sydney

For Kay Jerman, in appreciation

ISBN 0-590-41660-X

Text copyright © 1982 by Steven Kroll. Illustrations copyright © 1982 by Janet Stevens. All rights reserved. This edition published by Scholastic Inc., 730 Broadway, New York, NY 10003, by arrangement with Holiday House, Inc.

12   6/9

Printed in the U.S.A   08

Wilbur was very big and very tall. He had great big ears and great big feet.

And that was why he was chosen to be the Easter Bunny. He was strong enough to carry lots of baskets of Easter eggs. His legs were long enough for him to cross a road in a single hop. And because he delivered his eggs the night before Easter, he never had to worry about being seen.

Everyone knows you're not supposed to see the Easter Bunny.

This Easter, Wilbur had done all his work early. He'd woven lots of new wicker baskets. He'd dyed the Easter eggs and painted them with pretty designs. He'd made lots of jelly beans and chocolate candy. Everything was ready to deliver. Only on Easter Eve, Wilbur got sick.

His head was stuffed up, and his nose was runny. His throat was sore, and he had a temperature. His eyes were red, and his ears hurt.

Wilbur lay on his bed and groaned. Who was going to deliver the Easter baskets?

Hours went by. It was getting very late. Wilbur's rabbit friends came and banged on his door.

"Wilbur!" shouted Hector. "Wilbur, you have to get going!"

"Wilbur!" shouted Francine. "Wilbur, it's after midnight!"

"Wilbur!" shouted Charles and Henrietta, "Wilbur, if you don't go soon, the children won't have any Easter eggs!"

"I know," moaned Wilbur. "But I can't get up. I'm too sick."

Wilbur's friends banged on the door some more. But Wilbur felt too awful to listen. He took some more medicine, rolled over, and fell back asleep.

Charles and Henrietta talked things over with Hector and Francine. Something had to be done. If Wilbur wasn't going to deliver the Easter eggs, they would have to deliver them for him.

Hector and Francine loaded themselves up with Easter baskets. Charles and Henrietta did the same. The baskets were so heavy, they could hardly walk.

The four of them struggled through the woods.
"Hector," said Francine, "Hector, I can hardly see!"
"That's all right," said Hector, "just try to follow me,
Francine."

At that moment Francine bumped into Hector, and Charles bumped into Henrietta. Dozens of Easter baskets crashed to the ground. Broken eggs were everywhere.

"I think," said Charles, "we'll have to think of a different idea."

He and Henrietta went to get her red wagon. Hector and Francine helped them load it with Easter baskets. When it was piled high, all four of them pulled the wagon to the road.

Suddenly the wagon hit a rock and turned over. The Easter baskets were scattered everywhere.

"I don't think we can do this," said Hector.

"Soon it will be morning," said Charles.

"We'll have to make Wilbur get up," said Henrietta.

When his four rabbit friends got back to his burrow,
Wilbur was still asleep. As they pounded on his door again,
he opened one eye.

"Wilbur!" shouted Charles, "Wilbur, you have to deliver
the eggs yourself!"

"Wilbur!" shouted Francine. "Wilbur, there isn't much
time left!"

Wilbur lay in bed, grumbling. He blew his nose and
coughed.

Hector and Francine ran into the burrow and dumped
Wilbur on the floor.

"All right," he said, "all right, I'm coming."

He put on his earmuffs, his scarf, and his favourite jacket to make sure he kept warm. He put an ice pack on his head, a nice, big handkerchief in his jacket pocket, and tucked a hot water bottle under his arm.

"Hurry!" his friends shouted. "Hurry, Wilbur!"

Wilbur shuffled to the door. "I'm going to do this because it's my duty," he said, "but you're going to have to help me."

"Of course," said Hector.

"Certainly," said Francine.

"We're your friends!" said Charles and Henrietta.

Together they helped Wilbur load himself up with Easter baskets. In a moment there were baskets up and down his legs and around his ears. Finally he was ready.

Wilbur struggled out into the woods, with his friends pulling the red wagon behind him. He knew he'd have to hurry. It was almost daylight.

But his joints ached, and his head hurt. His nose was running, and his cough was getting worse.

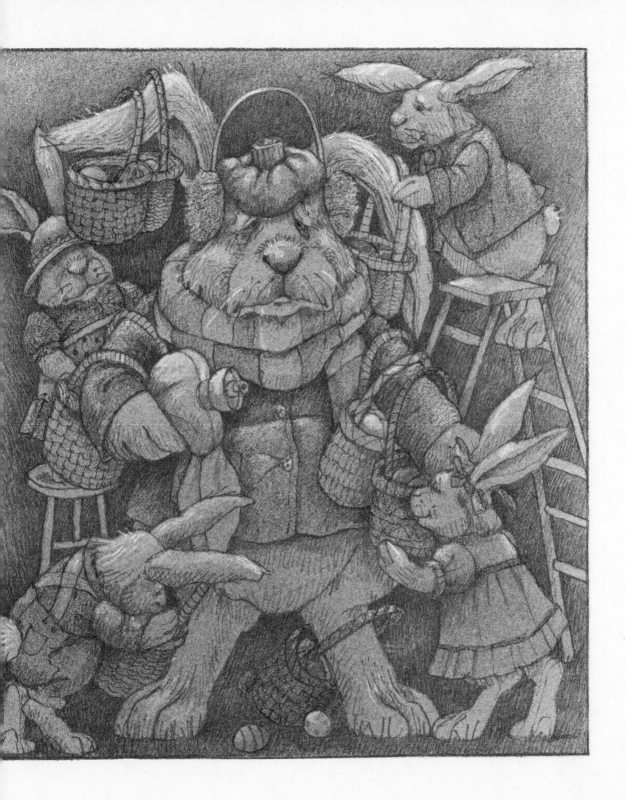

He thumped up to the first house. Everyone was fast asleep. He left two baskets of eggs on the front doorstep.

So far, so good. At the next house, he crept inside and left a basket by a little boy's bed.

When he got outside, the sun was rising. And a paper
boy was cycling into the drive!

Wilbur froze. He was much too tired to run. The boy
was sure to see him!

At that moment Francine jumped up and grabbed the newspaper out of the boy's hands. She tossed it to Hector, and the two of them thumped off across the yard.

"Hey!" yelled the boy. "Come back with that newspaper!" And he ran after Hector and Francine, allowing plenty of time for Wilbur to escape.

When the group was back together and Wilbur had
caught his breath, he thanked Hector and Francine for saving
him. But before he knew it, he was in trouble again.

Three houses later, he was leaving a little girl's room when he had to sneeze. He reached for his handkerchief, but not in time to prevent a huge ACHOO. The little girl sat up.

Wilbur dived under the bed. His ears and his feet stuck
out. Any second he'd be seen. Then Charles and Henrietta
pulled the covers over the little girl's head. Wilbur jumped
up and ran out of the house. That had been close!

But Wilbur's troubles were not over.

"Hurry! Hurry! Hide behind that tree!" shouted Charles
as a woman and her dog began to chase him.

"Hurry! Hurry! Jump into that bush!" shouted Hector
as he and Charles distracted a policeman.

"Quick! Under that sheet!" shouted the four bunnies
as a man reached out to pick up his milk.

With so much hiding and diving to do, Wilbur left a lot of his baskets in very odd places. But finally they were all delivered. Wilbur was so tired, he fell asleep. His friends had to pull him home in the red wagon.

When the children started looking for their Easter baskets, they found them under bushes, on fenceposts, and hanging from trees. It was the strangest Easter they'd ever had, but they didn't mind. Easter had never been so much fun!